ADVENTURES OF

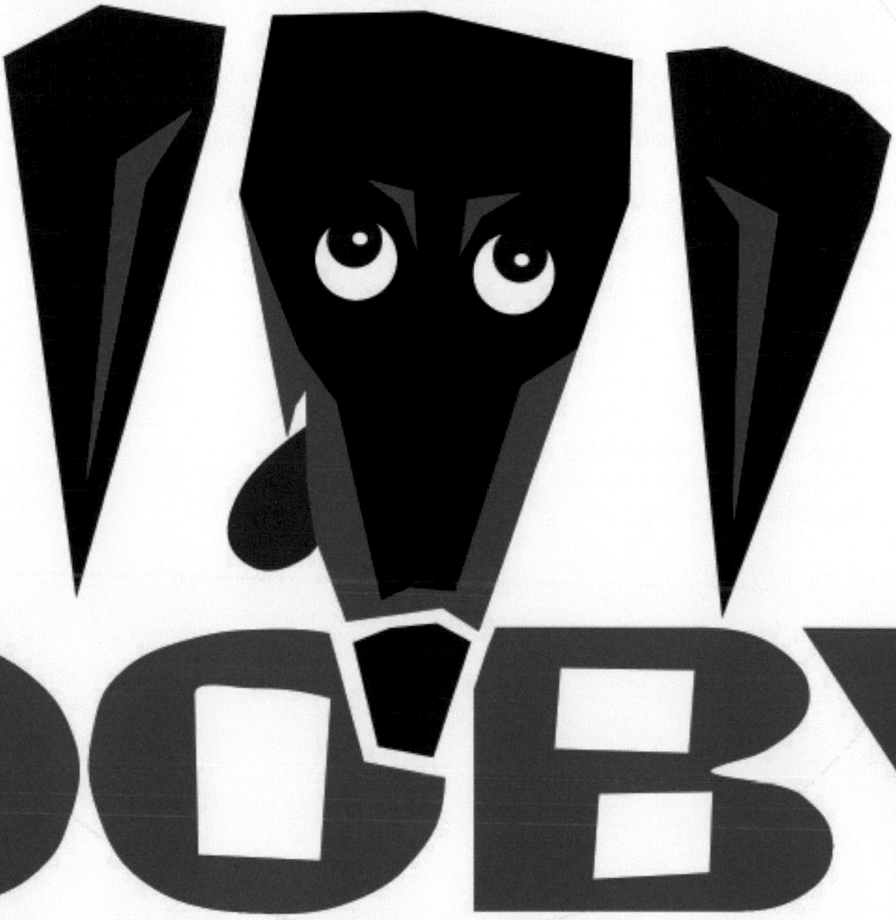

DOBY

"The Little Wiener Dog"

AuthorHouse™
1663 Liberty Drive
Bloomington, IN 47403
www.authorhouse.com
Phone: 833-262-8899

Because of the dynamic nature of the Internet, any web addresses or links contained in this book may have changed
since publication and may no longer be valid. The views expressed in this work are solely those of the author and do
not necessarily reflect the views of the publisher, and the publisher hereby disclaims any responsibility for them.

Any people depicted in stock imagery provided by Getty Images are models,
and such images are being used for illustrative purposes only.
Certain stock imagery © Getty Images.

This book is printed on acid-free paper.

ISBN: 978-1-4343-5347-4 (sc)

Library of Congress Control Number: 2008900203

Print information available on the last page.

Published by AuthorHouse 03/16/2021

authorHOUSE®

ADVENTURES OF

DOBY

"The Little Wiener Dog"

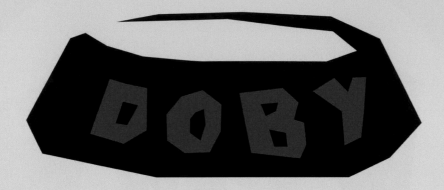

For Doby my little granddog and his family Randy, Cindy, T.J., Zack, and Chase.

Special thanks
To Brett, my nephew for his
artistic illustrations.

To Jennifer for her help.

This is a story about my little granddog **DOBY**.

Doby a Dachshund (in German, means "badger dog"), is a breed of hunting dog having short legs, a long body, and long ears. Originally developed in Germany, dachshunds were used to drive badgers from their holes, because of their short legs. Seldom used for hunting today, they are valued as pets for their bravery and good disposition. In addition, because of their long body and short legs, they have the nickname "wiener dog."

DOBY'S Adventures Began...

...On a warm summer day in
August. Three excited boys
went running outside as
mom's van drove into the driveway.
Mom opened the door of the van, and there,
on a little blanket, was the cutest, tiniest,
little black puppy. His neck was a tan color,
and he had four tan paws.

The puppy looked
up at the boys and
started wagging
his tail. He jumped
up from the
blanket and
started licking
their faces. He was so excited to have not
one, but three boys to play with. The boys
each had their turn, along with dad, holding
the very excited puppy. The little puppy
thought they are so nice; I am going to have
a great home!

They decided to give the puppy a name. One of the boys, Chase, the youngest remembered he had a little stuffed toy dog named Doby that actually looked like the puppy. They all agreed Doby would be the puppy's name.

Doby soon became accustomed to his name and new home. He liked to run all over the house. In fact, everyone had to be care-ful not to step on him; he was so small and always underneath their feet. House training

Doby, to go outside for his bathroom chores was a bit of chore itself. It took some time before he learned to go to the door and bark when he needed out. Doby was now a big part of the family and almost forgot he was a dog. Mrs. Carey the boys' mom was fascinated that he had his own little blanket, which he carried around and would nap with. Doby liked sleeping in bed with whichever boy would let him. He had another favorite place to sleep: with dad in his recliner chair, sometimes on his lap or snuggled beside him.

Please?

The boys taught him to do many tricks. Doby could sit on his hind legs and beg for his treat. He could also roll over and play dead. Another smart thing they taught him was crawl across the floor. Doby was a very smart dog.

T.J., the oldest boy, would tease Doby and make him jealous by taking the little toy dog and pretending to pet and talk to it. Doby began to whine and jump on him. T.J. would pick Doby up, cuddle him, and say, "I still love you Doby. Here is your favorite blanket." Doby took his blanket, and found a place to lie. Everything was all right with Doby again.

DOBY FINDS HIS WAY HOME

Doby went with the family on a visit to Grandpa and Grandma Dudley's. When they arrived, Doby was very excited he knew there would be treats, or num nums, as Grandma Dudley called them. On this particular visit,

the boys were outside playing with Doby, and at the edge of the woods, there was a little squirrel making noises. The little squirrel was yelling at Doby, saying, "Hey little dog! Your legs are so short; I bet you can't catch me." At the little squirrel's teasing, Doby ran into the woods to catch that squirrel.

He loved chasing after squirrels, or any little animal, especially cats. This time he really wanted to catch that little squirrel. As the little squirrel ran from behind a big tree, he yelled at Doby, "Hey little dog! Here I am! Bet you can't catch me." Then he darted behind another tree.

Doby ran very fast to the tree, but
no squirrel. "Where did that little squirrel
go? I bet he climbed another tree." Then Doby
heard a noise and ran further in the woods.
"What was that? Maybe that little squirrel is
over there."

With all the little animals running and rustling
the leaves, Doby just kept going. He would

get so excited when there was something to chase. Doby got tired of all the running and found a pile of leaves to lie on and rest. He soon fell asleep. When the little squirrel found Doby sleeping, he decided to take a rest, close enough to keep an eye on Doby.

He awoke to someone calling his name, sounds like Chase, one of his buddies. He thought I had better go back, it is getting late. "Oh no there goes that little squirrel, I'll catch him this time." The little squirrel just laughed at him "Ha ha you can't catch me little dog, I'm too fast for you." Doby ran and

ran but the little squirrel was fast, and he could hide very well. While Doby was still chasing the squirrel, his family was calling for him, but Doby did not pay any attention to them. He was having too much fun with the little squirrel. The family kept calling for Doby, but he never came back. Mr. Carey, the boy's dad, decided they had to leave Doby at Grandma and Grandpa Dudley's house, and would pick him up the next day.

When Doby was tired of chasing the squirrel, he remembered his family calling for him. The sun was setting, and it was beginning to get dark. Since dogs can see in the dark, Doby did not really need the moonlight to see, even though there was a full moon.

When Doby ran out of the woods, he was expecting to find his family, but they were not there. He put his nose to the ground and soon picked up their scent. He began following the scent down the road. He ran down the gravel road towards the main road where cars, trucks, and all kinds of vehicles were driving by. "Hmmm what did Zack (one of the boys) say before we would cross the road? I remember!" he said. "We have to look both ways. Make sure there were no cars coming." Doby hesitated, and thought, "I have to be careful crossing this road."

Just then, the little squirrel jumped from a tree, and asked, "What is wrong little dog?" Doby answered, "My family left me, and I should have listened to them when they called for me. Now, I have to find my way home, and I don't know how far it is." The little squirrel said, "I'm sorry, I caused you to miss them, but we were having so much fun. You know, I play in these woods all the time. Maybe I can help."

My name is Joey. What is your name, little dog with the short legs?" Doby answered, "My legs may be short, but I can still run fast, and my name is Doby." The little squirrel said, "Don't be angry. I am sorry, I was only teasing." Doby said, "That's ok, but it isn't nice to make fun of someone." Joey said, "Yeh, you're right. Come on, let's get going." Doby started sniffing the air and said, "Right let's go."

Doby and Joey made sure there were no cars coming when they crossed the road and continued through the woods.

They had gone just a little ways when they heard, "Hooty hoot! Who are you?" Doby said, "What was that?" Joey answered "Oh that is Hooty the Owl." To Hooty, he said, "This is Doby, my new friend. You see we played too long in the woods, and his family left him; now I'm helping him find his way home."

Then Doby said, "Yes, I really need to get home. I miss my family, and they will be so worried."

READY OR NOT...HERE I COME!

Hooty the Owl said, "Oh, yes. I remember you; I have been to your house before, watching you and the boys playing hide and seek at night." Doby then remembered hearing the hooty hoot sounds before and said, "I've heard your sounds before, but didn't know that it was you." Hooty replied, "You were having so much fun; I just liked watching and did not tell you who I was." Hooty asked, "Would you like for me to show you the way?" "Yes, please do." Doby answered.

Hooty the Owl would fly a ways and make his sounds for Doby and Joey to follow. With Hooty showing them the way Doby was home in no time. Doby told his new friends thank you and please come back sometime. As Joey and Hooty left they said they would. Doby ran to the back door and started to bark. "I'm home! Let me in."

T.J., Zack, and Chase had been getting ready for bed and wishing Doby was home when they heard the barking. Chase was the first one to get to the door, and when he opened it, there was **Doby.** Doby ran inside and started jumping all over the boys and thinking he was glad to be home with his family. Next time when they called him, he would be sure to listen.

DOBY GOES FISHING

It was a beautiful spring day. The temperature was just right: no jackets, just shirt sleeves. The birds were chirping, and the little squirrels were jumping from limb to limb. Grandma had gone outside to do a little yard work but soon changed her mind. She looked down at their little lake and could see the fish jumping in the water. It had been a long winter, and it was such a fine day to go fishing.

Doby's family was not at home, and Doby did not like being home without them. Therefore, he did what he would usually do when they were gone. He went to Grandpa and Grandma Carey's house, since they only lived a short distance up the road. He loved getting treats from grandma; and they have three cats for Doby to chase. Oh, what fun he would have!

MEEEEEEOOOOOOOOOOOOOOW...

MEEEEEEOOOOOOOOOOOOOOW...

Grandma was outside, and Doby went running to her. Grandma said, "Hello Doby Doo! I guess you came for your treat today, right?" "I am sure I can handle that, but you will have to wait a minute." "Didn't you find any of the cats to chase today?" Doby looked up at her and thought, "No, I didn't find the cats, but I would really like a treat. Come on, grandma." He kept whining and running around her.

RUFF...RUFF!

Doby kept following Grandma everywhere, begging for his treat. Grandma said, "Okay Doby I will give you a treat, but you will have to perform for me." Grandma held the treat up and told Doby to speak, which he replied with a bark. Then Doby began doing all his tricks on his own. He sat on his hind legs, and then he rolled over and played dead. Grandma said, "Oh Doby what a smart dog you are."

Then grandma said, "Doby, I was going fishing. Why don't you go with me, and keep me company?" Doby seemed to understand and followed Grandma as she got her fishing pole.

As they were walking to the little lake, Doby was getting so excited, wondering what Grandma was going to do. He was running all around, making little whining noises.

He never left Grandma's side
watching everything she did. When she
threw the lure in the water, Doby was trying
to go after it. Grandma said "Doby, you can't
do that. Just be patient wait and see what I get.
Grandma reeled the lure back in, but no fish. Doby
just looked at the lure, his tail wagging, and then
looked out at the water. He started whining again.
Grandma said, "Ok, Doby. I'm going to throw it

back in the water, just give me time." Then she threw the lure in the water.

Grandma felt the fish as it took the lure, "Doby! I have a fish." Doby was watching the water and saw the fish jump up out of the water. He got very excited and started jumping on Grandma and going toward the water's edge. When grandma reeled the fish in, Doby smelled the fish and watched as Grandma took it off the lure and threw it back in the water.

Grandma said to Doby,
"Want me to do it again?"
Doby started whining and jumping
on Grandma and running in the
water. "Ok. Here I go Doby."
She threw the lure in the
water again, at least two
more times, before she
caught another fish.
Doby again was so excited, watching the water where
the fish was coming from. Grandma and Doby
walked around the little lake fishing, most of the

afternoon. Doby heard a squirrel making a noise and wondered if it was the little squirrel Joey, his new friend. He ran up to the tree and said, "Hey Joey is that you?" Joey answered, "It's me Doby, and I've been watching you and grandma throwing something in the water." "What are you doing?" Doby answered, "It's called fishing, and grandma told me I was a good fishing buddy. It is a lot of fun." Doby then asked Joey where Hooty the Owl was. Joey said, "Hooty was up too late last night and was still sleeping today. I will tell him about your fishing."

Just then, they noticed Grandma was walking towards them.

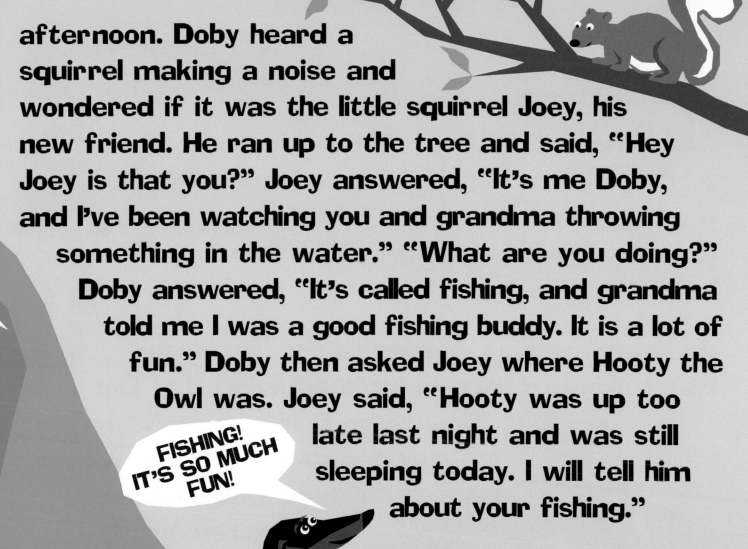

Grandma said to Doby, "I have to go back to the house and get some work done. I bet the boys are home from school and wondering where you are Doby Doo. You better go home."

As grandma was walking to the house, she was talking to herself. "It is amazing that Doby likes to go fishing. I don't know of any dog that likes to go fishing except Doby. He really gets excited, waiting for me to catch a fish." Then she yelled, "Come on Doby Doo lets go."

Doby told Joey, Grandma was right. The boys would be home from school, he had better go. Joey said, "Doby I hope you know how very lucky you are to have such a wonderful family." As Doby turned to leave he answered, "I do know Joey,"

"See ya."

THE END.

Printed in the United States
by Baker & Taylor Publisher Services